THE LONG ROAD HOME

THE
LONG ROAD
HOME

*A Tale of Two Sons and
a Father's Never-Ending Love*

Written by SARAH WALTON   *Illustrated by* CHRISTINA YANG

CROSSWAY®

WHEATON, ILLINOIS

Illustrations, book design, and cover design: Christina Yang

First printing 2024

Printed in China

ISBN: 978-1-4335-8891-4

Library of Congress Cataloging-in-Publication Data

Names: Walton, Sarah, 1984– author. | Yang, Christina K., illustrator.

Title: The long road home : a tale of two sons and a father's never-ending love / by Sarah Walton; illustrated by Christina Yang.

Description: Wheaton, Illinois : Crossway, [2024] | Audience: Ages 6–8

Identifiers: LCCN 2024007312 | ISBN 9781433588914 (hardcover)

Subjects: LCSH: Prodigal son (Parable)—Juvenile literature. | Bible stories, English—Juvenile literature. | Jesus Christ—Parables—Juvenile literature.

Classification: LCC BT378.P8 W243 2024 | DDC 226.8—dc23/eng/20240315

LC record available at https://lccn.loc.gov/2024007312

Crossway is a publishing ministry of Good News Publishers.

RRDS			35	34	33	32	31	30	29	28	27	26	25
15	14	13	12	11	10	9	8	7	6	5	4	3	2	1

For Ben, Hannah, Haley, and Eli.
Wherever your journey may take you,
I pray it leads you to the grace, forgiveness,
and joy that is only found in Jesus.
For that is where you truly belong.
Love, Mom

PART 1

The Land of Belonging

IN THE PEACEFUL LAND OF BELONGING, there lived a father and his two sons, Wander and Goodness.

As Wander and Goodness grew up, they had everything they needed. Alongside their father, they worked hard to take care of their family's property and often heard him say, "God has given us this land. May we be good stewards of what he's given us." They were cared for, provided for, and loved.

But one day when Wander was doing his chores, he stopped and sighed. He looked off into the distance and began to wonder, "Isn't there something better out there for me? I love my father, but I want to be free to do what I want. I want to be happy!"

Suddenly, he had an idea! Wander remembered something his father had told him and his brother. "One day, my sons, you will be given your part of all I own." But Wander didn't want to wait any longer. He wanted his money now! Maybe this was the ticket he needed to leave his home and have the freedom he wanted to find what would make him happy.

So Wander hatched a plan. He went to his father and demanded all the money he had been promised.

With a look of sadness in his eyes, his father gave Wander the money set aside for him. But with it, he said, *"Wherever you go, my son, I want you to remember that I love you with a never-ending love."*

As Wander felt the money in his hands, he barely heard his father's words. His thoughts swirled with excitement. He quickly packed his bag and daydreamed about the journey that lay ahead.

If there was something better out there, he was sure to find it.

Goodness watched his brother's figure fade into the distance
and muttered to himself, "What a foolish brother. I'm better than
that. Good thing my father has me for a son, since I would never be
so selfish."

PART 2

Wander's Journey

WANDER TRAVELED FAR AND WIDE, across rushing rivers and over rolling hills. He did exactly what he wanted and enjoyed his newfound freedom. Though at times he thought he heard his father's voice, warning him about choices he knew he wouldn't like, Wander pushed those thoughts aside.

Eventually, Wander came upon the beautiful town of Perfection. As he walked its streets, Wander liked what he saw. No one seemed to make a mistake or fail at anything. Everything was done just right. But no one even seemed to notice him. Everyone hustled and bustled around the town, wonderful and busy. But Wander didn't notice their exhausted faces and empty eyes.

Wander knew he wasn't perfect, but he really wanted people to like him. So he did all he could to look perfect, just like all the other townspeople. But soon he grew frustrated and upset with himself whenever he made mistakes. Instead of finding happiness in Perfection, the town left him tired and sad. So Wander decided to travel on, searching for something more.

For weeks he wandered the countryside, growing tired, hungry, and dirty. One day, he rowed across a glistening lake and followed a winding road until he finally reached another town, the beautiful city of Prosperity. Wander's eyes grew big with amazement! Everywhere he looked, men and women wore the finest clothes, ate the best food, and showed off their newest gadgets. When he looked down at his worn shoes and dirty clothes, he grew embarrassed and tried to hide before anyone saw him.

Then Wander found a street full of stores. He stopped at shop after shop, pulling out his bag of money in each one and buying only the best. Each time he bought something new, he felt a wave of excitement and confidence come over him. But it didn't take long before the feelings faded. And whenever he noticed someone walk by with something better, he always had to have it too.

Before long, Wander grew
tired, weighed down by all the
extra clothes, toys, and gadgets
he now carried around with him.
As he neared the edge of the town,
the only thing that seemed to
feel lighter was his bag of money.
Instead of finding happiness in
Prosperity, the city left him feeling
empty inside. *Surely there must
be something else that can make
me happy*, he thought.
So he traveled on.

PART 3

Lost and Alone

WANDER NOTICED A STRANGE EMPTINESS growing inside of him, but he was determined to find a place to belong. So he kept walking, far away from home. Soon Wander came upon the exciting town of Popularity. As he looked around, everyone seemed to be important and impressive. Some were showing off their talents to a cheering crowd; some were making people laugh; some were displaying their new inventions; and some were the most beautiful people he'd ever seen.

As Wander walked through the streets, he wanted to find a way he could fit in. Did he have any talents? Was he funny enough to make people laugh? Was he smart enough to impress anyone? Would his new clothes and gadgets make him draw crowds like everyone else?

While Wander desperately tried to think of a way to stand out, he noticed a man sitting on a bench. He looked sad, with a lonely expression on his face. Wander called out, "Sir, why are you so sad?" The man looked up with empty eyes and replied, "I no longer have any purpose here. I was once the funniest man in town, but someone funnier than me came along. And I've now been forgotten."

Wander felt a lump grow in his throat. *Would he, too, be forgotten and alone if he couldn't find a way to be talented, funny, or smart enough? Maybe he wouldn't have any value either.*

Instead of finding happiness in the town of Popularity, Wander was feeling lost and unlovable. As he left the city, he heard his father's words echo in his mind. *Wherever you go, my son, I want you to remember that I love you with a never-ending love.* But Wander quickly pushed his words aside, determined to find his own way.

He walked under the darkness of night until he reached the village of Desperation. It was a sad-looking place. Men and women made fun of those around them and stole whatever they wanted. Even in the dark, everyone looked angry and unhappy. Out of fear of the townspeople, he quickly got rid of his fine clothes and expensive items to avoid being noticed. Wander didn't like it there, but he needed to eat before continuing his journey. He went into an inn to buy some food. But when he reached into his money bag, all he felt was . . . nothing. In a panic, he turned the bag inside out. There had to be more! But no, there wasn't a coin to be found.

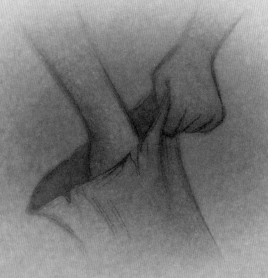

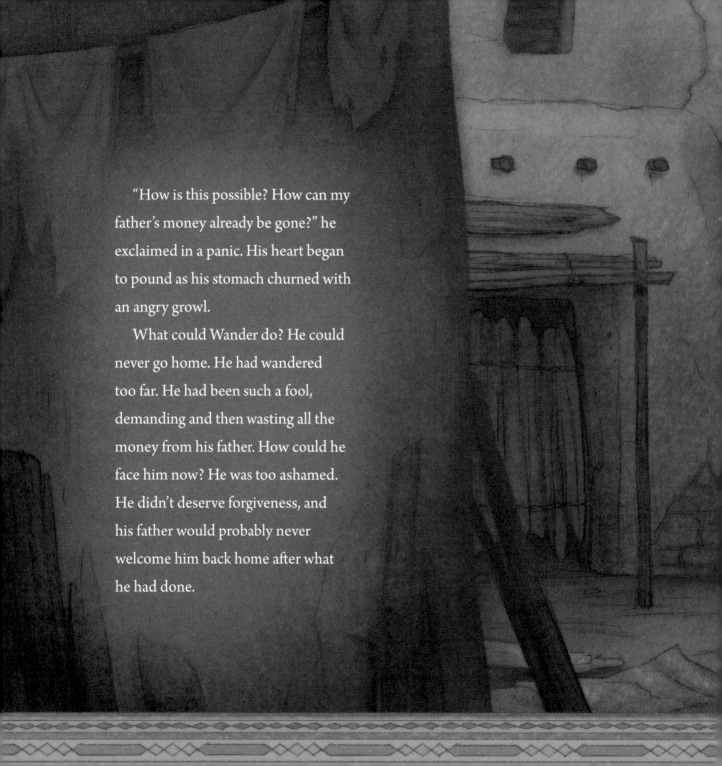

"How is this possible? How can my father's money already be gone?" he exclaimed in a panic. His heart began to pound as his stomach churned with an angry growl.

What could Wander do? He could never go home. He had wandered too far. He had been such a fool, demanding and then wasting all the money from his father. How could he face him now? He was too ashamed. He didn't deserve forgiveness, and his father would probably never welcome him back home after what he had done.

PART 4

The Road Home

SAD, HUNGRY, ASHAMED, AND ALONE in the village of
Desperation, Wander begged the townspeople for a job and a
place to stay. No one helped him until, finally, a local farmer sent
him to feed the pigs in his field. But still he had nothing to eat.
Before long, Wander's hunger grew so unbearable that he begged
to eat the mushy, smelly food that he fed to the pigs. When the
farmer refused, Wander fell down among the pigs and wept.

In this town of Desperation, Wander was truly desperate.

Suddenly, his father's words rang in his ears loud and clear. *Remember that I love you with a never-ending love.*

Although he was ashamed, and he knew he deserved nothing from his father, Wander felt a small ray of hope. If he went home and begged for forgiveness . . . if his father really *did* love him with a never-ending love . . . then maybe, just maybe, his father would hire him to work (and eat) just like one of his hired servants.

Wander stood up, dropped his bags (he knew they would only weigh him down), and took off as fast as his tired legs would take him. He traveled a long time. Back through the town of Popularity, back through the town of Prosperity, back through the town of Perfection, over rolling hills and across rushing rivers, and to the edge of his father's land.

There he sat down to catch his breath and think of what he would say to his father.

But before he could finish his thought, he saw a figure in the distance, waving his arms and yelling something that Wander could barely make out. The person was running! As he grew closer, Wander heard the voice of his father calling out, *"My son, my son!"*

Wander froze, afraid of what might happen next. What would his father do to him?

PART 5

The Celebration

WANDER WATCHED HIS FATHER run straight toward him. Before he knew it, his father reached him and threw his arms around him. Wander collapsed into his strong, compassionate, and loving arms.

Still shocked by his father's embrace, Wander exclaimed, "Father, I'm so sorry! I have sinned against you and against God. I was foolish and thought something else would make me happy. But with you, I had everything I needed all along."

Wander stood up straight and looked in his father's eyes. "Please, I know I don't deserve anything from you. Would you show me mercy and hire me as one of your workers?"

To his surprise, his father's face beamed! Then he laughed—
a rich laugh full of joy! He called to his workers: "Bring Wander the
finest clothes and shoes! And prepare a feast of only the best food!
This calls for a celebration!"

His father turned to Wander and said, "My son, you were lost,
but you have now returned home. You were once searching for
something better, but you have returned to where you belonged
all along—the place where true joy is found."

Wander could not look at his father as tears ran down his face. His father put his arm around him. "You are valuable in my eyes not because you're good enough, talented enough, successful enough, or likable enough, but because you are my son. And you are loved with a never-ending love. All that is mine is yours."

As Wander and his father walked to the house, all the workers prepared for the celebration. Everyone was excited. This would be a feast like no other!

But when Wander's brother, Goodness, heard about his father's celebration for Wander, he grew angry. *How unfair that my father would celebrate this brother's return. Wasn't he the foolish one? Don't I deserve the celebration? Haven't I been the better son?* In his anger, Goodness refused to celebrate his brother's coming home.

When the father heard about Goodness's reaction, he went out to encourage him to join the party. "Come inside, my son, and enjoy the feast. Together—you, me, and Wander—this is where you belong."

But Goodness exclaimed, "How can you celebrate my brother after all he did? You've never given me a celebration after how good I've been!"

His father looked at Goodness with kindness in his eyes, put his arm around him, and gently replied, "Son, you are loved not because of what you have or haven't done for me, but because you're my child. All that I have has always been yours.

"But your brother, who once was wandering and lost, has now been found. And *that* is worth celebrating."

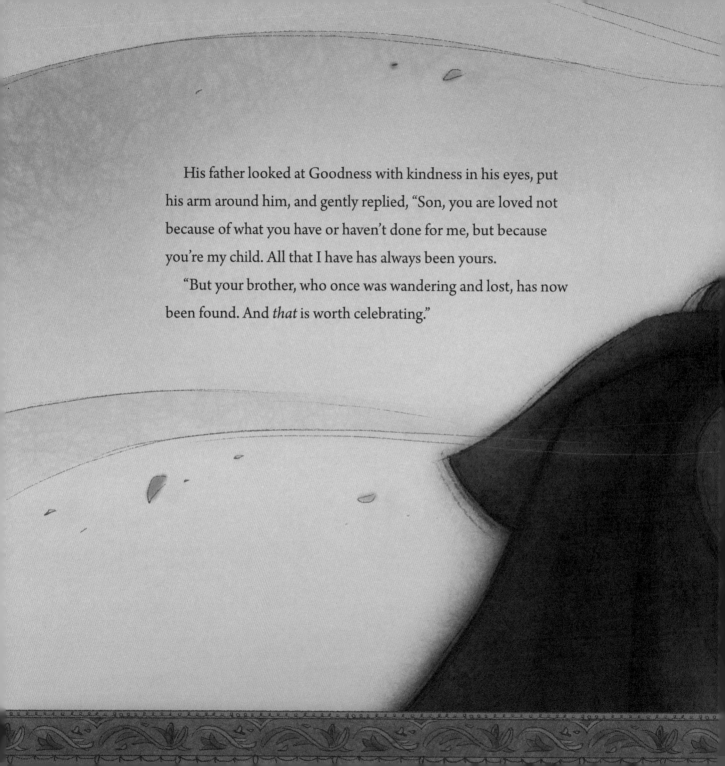

NOTE FOR PARENTS

Children (and adults) today often hear the message that they should do whatever feels good, whatever will make them happy. As parents, it's important to help our children see beyond the surface of behaviors, choices, and circumstances. We should take time to help them evaluate what untruths, motives, and beliefs lie beneath the surface.

I hope this story, combining elements of John Bunyan's *The Pilgrim's Progress* and Jesus's parable of the prodigal son, launches many conversations with your children. In my own home, I have found that conversations often trace back to one of the themes represented by the towns Wander explores or to the pride of his brother, Goodness.

Discussing these unique struggles leads to the answers that are found only within the hope of Christ. Because of this gospel hope, at the end of our best days—and our worst—stands our heavenly Father, with a heart ready to forgive and arms ready to receive.